CRYSTAL'S CHANCE

SUSANNAH BRIN

Artesian Press

P.O. Box 355, Buena Park, CA 90621

Take Ten Books
Romance

Other Take Ten Themes:

Mystery
Sports
Adventure
Chillers
Thrillers
Disaster
Horror
Fantasy

Project Editor: Dwayne Epstein
Assistant Editor: Molly Mraz
Illustrations: Fujiko
Graphic Design: Tony Amaro
©2003 Artesian Press

www.artesianpress.com

 Artesian **Press**   ISBN 1-58659-459-1

CONTENTS

Chapter 1

Crystal Diaz stared out the window of the pickup truck. Huge, grassy green meadows stretched for miles on both sides of the highway. There were tears in Crystal's dark eyes as they passed a large horse farm with neatly painted barns and miles of white fences. Giant metal sprinklers sprayed streams of water across newly cut fields.

It's good to be going home, Crystal thought. She took a deep breath to keep from crying. Six months in the hospital had seemed like forever. Now it was over, and she was going home.

She looked down at the nylon-and-plastic brace on her left leg. Again, tears stung her eyes. She shook her head and bit her lip. *I have to stop this crying*, Crystal told herself.

Miguel Diaz looked at his daughter. He saw her look at the brace on her leg. He felt sad for her. He remembered the accident, too. "The doctors said you won't always have to wear a brace, sweetheart," Miguel said. He turned his attention back to his driving.

"Maybe not, but I'll always have a limp," Crystal said.

Miguel Diaz frowned. "Maybe not. Anyway, a limp isn't so bad. You were lucky you weren't killed or hurt so badly that you'd never walk again."

"Easy for you to say. You walk just fine," Crystal said. She was angry and felt sorry for herself.

Miguel sighed. He was not sure how to deal with his daughter's changing moods. The accident had damaged more than her leg.

Crystal shuddered, thinking about the accident. She couldn't stop thinking about it. She kept seeing it over and over in her mind. She was on her horse, Chance. They had reached the river. She made him jump by squeezing her legs into his sides. As the horse took off from the muddy bank, Crystal realized her mistake.

It was too late. Swollen from the spring runoff, the river was too wide. Chance couldn't reach the far bank. Missing the target, he lost his footing on the moss-covered rocks. Slipping and falling to his knees, Chance tried to pull himself up. He fell over, trapping Crystal against a boulder.

Her left leg was broken and terribly crushed. Now metal pins and a brace held it together. *I shouldn't have asked him to jump. It was my fault. I didn't look*, she thought sadly.

Crystal rolled down the window. She hoped the warm summer air would calm her. It didn't. She was as jumpy as a racehorse in the starting gate.

Miguel smiled at his daughter, hoping to make her feel better. "Everything will be better now, you'll see. Donya's been cooking your favorite foods all week."

Crystal nodded, imagining her aunt in the kitchen with plates and platters of food all around her. Aunt Donya was Crystal's mother's older sister. She'd come to live with them when Crystal's mother died years ago. She never left. "Why didn't you ever marry Donya after Mother died?" Crystal asked, suddenly curious.

Miguel shook his head and smiled. "Donya is twenty years older than I am. Besides, your mother, Carmen, was the only woman for me. Don't get me wrong. I'm grateful for all Donya has done for us, but gratitude is all I feel."

"I bet you'd miss her cooking if she

left," Crystal teased.

"Sure. No one can cook Cuban food like your Aunt Donya," grinned Miguel, patting the small bulge around his waist.

"You still miss Cuba, don't you, Dad?"

Miguel nodded. "It was my country. I've lived here in Kentucky for twenty years now, but Cuba is still in my heart."

Crystal sighed and looked out the window again. "I guess I'll always feel that way about Kentucky, right?"

"Yes. Kentucky has always been your home. Speaking of home, we're almost there," Miguel said. He turned off the main highway onto a dirt road.

"I can't wait to see Chance. He's fine, isn't he? You weren't just *saying* he's okay?" Crystal asked. Her pretty face looked worried.

"No, he's fine. In fact, Leon has been walking him for you."

"Leon? Who's Leon?"

"Now, don't be getting yourself upset. Leon Ramirez is a young man from Florida. I hired him about a month ago," Miguel said. He turned his head so he wouldn't have to look into his daughter's eyes.

"You never told me," Crystal said. She knew they couldn't afford to hire anyone. She had always worked with the horses to help her father.

"I wanted to surprise you. Leon showed up one day needing a job. He came to America only a year ago, on a boat, just like I did twenty years ago."

Crystal looked at her father's deeply tanned face, waiting for him to explain how they could afford to hire help. Before the accident, she kept the farm's records and paid the bills. She knew how her father struggled every month to pay the bills.

Miguel shrugged his shoulders. "I know you're thinking we can't afford

Leon. But I couldn't turn away a countryman in need, could I?"

Crystal thought her father was too kind sometimes. He was always helping people. Then she understood. Her father had needed help when she was in the hospital and in rehab. Leon was probably the reason her father had been able to visit her so often.

Miguel stopped the pickup and got out. He opened the white gate that led to their house and horse barns. Crystal was excited. She couldn't wait to see her Aunt Donya and her horse, Chance.

Miguel got back in the truck. He grinned. "I think you're going to like Leon. You'll see. He's a big help."

Crystal frowned. She wasn't sure she would like Leon. Maybe she wasn't able to do all her chores yet, but she didn't want someone taking her place.

Chapter 2

"Darling girl!" cried Aunt Donya. She wrapped her arms around Crystal. "I've been counting the minutes all morning."

"It's good to see you, too, Auntie," Crystal said. She let the older woman touch her face and hair as if she were a doll.

"Come, you must rest from the long drive. And you must eat. You're too skinny," Aunt Donya said. She put her arm around Crystal's waist to help her walk into the house.

Crystal pushed her aunt away gently. "I can walk. I'm not a cripple." Turning, she didn't see the questioning look Donya gave Miguel. Nor did she see Miguel's shrug. What she did see was a tall, handsome young man about her own age leaning against the entrance to the stable. *Who does he think he is, looking at me like that?* Crystal thought.

"Oh, there's Leon," said Miguel. He had noticed that Crystal was staring at Leon. "I'll introduce you."

"No. Later. I'm tired now," Crystal lied. She limped toward the house, leaving Miguel and Donya to follow.

Crystal went into the long white house with its red-tiled floor, and limped straight to her bedroom. *Nothing has changed*, she thought, lying down on her quilt-covered bed.

The walls of her room were covered with pictures of horses. A bookcase was full of books, trophies, and bronze horse statues.

On the night table next to her bed was a picture of a pretty, dark-haired woman. Crystal picked up the picture.

"Hello, Mama. I'm back. I'm glad you're not here to see me limping around. I'm not your perfect girl anymore." Crystal's eyes filled with tears.

Hugging the photo of her mother, Crystal fell back on the bed and closed her eyes. Tears fell onto the white-ruffled pillowcase. *Everything's the same and different at the same time*, Crystal thought.

The late afternoon sun was streaming through the bedroom windows when Crystal woke up. She was surprised she had fallen asleep. She put the photo of her mother back on the night table. She swung her legs off the bed onto the floor. She stood up carefully, putting most of her weight on her good leg before shifting some to her left. *Will I always have to think like this?* she wondered as she limped down the hall toward the kitchen.

"Aunt Donya, why aren't you taking

your nap?" asked Crystal. She was surprised to see the older woman in the kitchen. For as long as Crystal could remember, her aunt had followed the Cuban custom of taking a nap in the afternoon.

Donya looked up from the cake she was covering with frosting. She laughed and shook her head. "I'm in this country fifteen years now. So the other day, I decided it's time to stop napping."

Crystal wondered if her aunt gave up the habit because of the accident. Aunt Donya had been taking a nap that day and woke up to the sound of sirens. Crystal could still remember her aunt's face, white with worry.

"Sit down and I'll fix you something to eat," said Donya.

"I'll wait until dinner. I'll just have some of these sugar cookies," Crystal said. She took a handful from a plate on the counter. "Is Dad outside?"

"No, I think he went to town. An errand or something," Donya said. She didn't look at Crystal when she spoke.

Crystal looked at her aunt for a moment and then walked to the door. "I think I'll go see Chance."

Donya's mouth closed tightly. She nodded her head, not saying a word as she turned back to the cake. Crystal knew her aunt thought she should wait and slowly ease back into life at the farm. Crystal felt that ever since the accident, all she'd been doing was easing back into life. Now she wanted to see her horse.

Crystal walked slowly toward the stable. She looked around at the farm. Nothing seemed to be changed since she left. The one-mile racetrack her father had made stood empty out beyond the first pasture. Several racehorses grazed in another fenced-in field.

She didn't recognize the two horses.

Must be boarders, she thought. She was surprised that there weren't more horses in the pasture. Usually, her father boarded six to ten horses this time of year. *Did business get worse while I was gone?* she wondered.

As Crystal entered the cool stable, several horses nickered. Two yearlings put their heads out of their stall doors as she passed. There were horse stalls on both sides of the long hallway of the barn. Most of the stalls were empty. *Not a good sign*, she thought.

Tiny bits of dust floated in the sunlight that shined through the windows and cracks in the walls of the barn. Crystal stopped near the last stall and gave a low whistle.

A beautiful black horse stuck its head out of the stall door. Its large, dark eyes seemed to open wider as it recognized her. It bobbed its head up and down and pawed the ground with its foot. "Hello, Chance. Hello, boy.

"Did you miss me?" asked Crystal. Chance licked
her hand as if to say, "Yes."

Did you miss me?" asked Crystal. She patted the horse's muzzle. The thoroughbred nibbled at Crystal's hair and snorted against her neck.

Crystal laughed and pulled strands of her hair from Chance's mouth. Leaning across the stall door, she checked her horse's body. There were no scars from the accident. Crystal sighed with relief.

Chance nudged his head against Crystal's shoulder, like he was pushing her to stand up straight. Again, Crystal laughed. "I know what you want," she said. She reached into her pocket for a lump of sugar.

"You shouldn't hand-feed your horse. You spoil him," said a heavily accented male voice.

Startled, Crystal jerked her head toward the voice. The young man she saw earlier, the one her father called Leon, stood only a few feet from her. "My horse is not spoiled," Crystal lied.

Leon smiled because he knew she was lying. "If he was mine, I would not hand-feed him. He'll think everyone has food in their hands. Do you want me to saddle him for you?"

Crystal stiffened. She wondered if Leon was teasing her. There was no way she would be riding Chance. Even thinking about it scared her.

"Not today," she said. She turned and started back to the house.

"Hey, I didn't mean to upset you," said Leon, following her. "I just thought he needs riding. I've only been hand-walking him."

Crystal turned and looked at Leon for a moment. He seemed like a nice boy. Suddenly, she felt foolish for being so sensitive. He didn't know she was scared of riding again. "Thank you for exercising him."

"No problem. We have not met. I'm Leon Ramirez," Leon said.

"I know," Crystal said. She liked

the way his smile made his whole face come alive with energy. She started walking again. She became aware of her limp.

"Maybe I could ride him for you?" Leon suggested. "I'm a great rider. In fact, tomorrow I ride your father's horse Havana Rose in a race against Mr. Rice's horse Southern Pride."

Crystal couldn't believe what she was hearing. She wondered why her father would race his favorite horse against Mr. Rice's horse. *Money*, thought Crystal. *My father needs money and he's willing to gamble for it*. "What time is the race, Leon?"

"At two o'clock on your father's track. Why? Are you going to come watch me ride?" Leon asked. He was smiling, but his dark eyes were watching her.

"You can count on it," Crystal said. She moved away, leaving Leon standing in the stable doorway.

Chapter 3

Crystal's father would not talk to her about the race at dinner or at breakfast the next morning. When Crystal tried to question Aunt Donya, the older woman just shook her head and went back into the kitchen.

Why won't anyone tell me what is going on? Crystal thought to herself. She crossed the paved driveway toward the stable. She could see her father hand-walking a gray yearling in the exercise arena. She looked around for Leon, but she did not see him anywhere.

Glad no one was watching, Crystal went quietly into her father's office. It was in a small, white building next to the stable. She quickly went to the computer and called up the farm's accounting files. There were no entries for the last six months.

Frowning, Crystal opened the desk drawer. Inside was a large stack of unpaid bills. She was looking at the mortgage bill when her father walked into the office.

"What are you doing in my desk?" Miguel asked. He walked toward her.

"Is this why you're racing Havana Rose? To pay the mortgage on the farm?" Crystal held up the bill.

Miguel looked worried. For a moment, he looked out the window at the horses grazing in the green fields. "Business has been bad these last few months. I got a little behind, and when Charley Rice suggested a race to clear the debt, I agreed."

Crystal felt angry. Over the years, she'd heard rumors about the bank president, Charley Rice. People said he liked to add to his horse farm by betting a rancher's debt against a special horse he wanted. "Oh, Daddy, isn't there another way?"

Miguel bowed his head like a guilty man. When he looked up, he smiled weakly. "Don't worry, sweetheart. Havana Rose is much faster than Southern Pride. Havana Rose will win and the debt will be crossed off the books."

"What if Havana Rose doesn't win, Daddy?" Crystal asked. Her voice got higher, as if she were talking to a child.

Miguel shrugged his shoulders. "Then Charley Rice will own Havana Rose and I will still owe the bank the mortgage money for the last six months. But don't worry, she will win. Remember how Havana Rose beat Mr. Wilson's horse only last year?"

"Yes, but I was riding her. Now you have Leon riding. Can he even ride?" Crystal asked. She couldn't stop herself from sounding angry.

"I can ride like the wind," Leon said, poking his head in the door.

Crystal frowned at Leon. She didn't like the way he always appeared from nowhere, like a cat hiding in the grass, ready to pounce.

"Mr. Rice and his son are here. They are out back unloading Southern Pride," Leon said.

Crystal's heart beat faster. She had not seen Bobby Lee Rice since her accident. He had called her and sent a card, but he never visited her at rehab. That had made her sad. She thought he liked her just as much as she liked him.

Outside, they saw Mr. Rice, Bobby Lee, and their horse-trailer driver, Carlos, holding the reins of a chestnut-colored horse, Southern Pride.

While her father and Leon walked toward Mr. Rice, Crystal stayed behind. She hated the idea of limping over to

Bobby Lee. She hated the thought that he might feel sorry for her.

When Bobby Lee saw her, he smiled and walked right over to her. "Crystal, it's good to see you," Bobby Lee said. He pushed a strand of blond hair off his forehead.

"You, too," answered Crystal coldly.

Bobby Lee stopped in front of her and looked into her eyes. He grinned. "You're not mad at me, are you?"

Crystal shook her head, making her long brown hair fly around her shoulders. "Why would I be mad, Bobby Lee?"

"I meant to get over to see you, but it seems like something always came up. You know my Daddy had me running chores for him all summer, and then the guys have been dragging me to some races." He grinned weakly, like he knew he didn't have a good excuse.

Crystal wanted to believe him. She

knew his father did make him work pretty hard. And he was always doing something with friends because everyone liked to be with Bobby Lee.

Still, she thought, *he could have visited once.* She couldn't help thinking that maybe he didn't want to do things with her now that she couldn't walk normally.

"Come on, Crystal, don't be mad. You know I'm just a good-old boy who doesn't always do the right thing," said Bobby Lee, making his Southern accent stronger than ever.

Crystal smiled. She couldn't help it. Bobby Lee was so charming that she just couldn't stay mad at him.

"Are you riding Havana Rose in the race today?" asked Bobby Lee.

Crystal stared at him. "Like I can ride with this brace on my leg. You are the most foolish person I know, Bobby Lee."

Bobby Lee shrugged. "I don't see

how a brace can stop you from riding once you're on the horse. That is, unless you're scared to get back in the saddle."

"I am not scared," Crystal said. "Leon Ramirez is riding." She started walking to the track where the others were already lining up the two horses. Bobby Lee walked alongside her.

"You're like an angry cat with its back up," he said. He was still teasing her.

Crystal stared at him, feeling anger rush through her body. "You don't visit me, you accuse me of being scared to ride, and your daddy is trying to steal my daddy's favorite horse just like he's done with other breeders. So how do you expect me to feel?"

Bobby Lee looked surprised and hurt. "My daddy isn't trying to steal anything. Maybe that accident of yours damaged your brain."

"My brain is just fine." Crystal

frowned at him. "I still know what is fair and decent, unlike you and your daddy."

Now it was Bobby Lee's turn to give her an angry look. Then he walked off toward the racetrack.

Crystal's angry words were out of her mouth before she could stop them. She quickly felt sorry for saying them.

Crystal watched as Bobby Lee mounted his father's horse. She looked at Leon, who was already on Havana Rose. Leon leaned forward in the saddle ready for the starter's signal. *He's got good form*, thought Crystal. She knew that good jockeys place their weight over the horse's center of gravity to reduce wind resistance and have better balance at high speed.

When the starter gun sounded, the horses sped forward in a burst of speed. "Come on, Havana Rose!" screamed Crystal.

The race was over in minutes. At

first, it seemed like Havana Rose would win. She was almost a full body length ahead, coming around the backstretch of the track. Then, suddenly, Havana Rose slowed to a trot. Southern Pride pounded over the finish line, yards ahead of Havana Rose.

Everyone was stunned, except for Mr. Rice. He was smiling and rubbing his hands together. With his sweaty red face, Crystal thought Mr. Rice looked happier than a pig in a mudhole.

Chapter 4

Something has to be wrong with Havana Rose, Crystal thought. She limped over to Leon and the horse. She heard Mr. Rice telling her father he'd take Havana Rose home today.

"What happened, Leon?" Crystal asked. She reached out to pat the horse's nose.

Leon shrugged. "I don't know. One minute we were flying like the wind, and the next she was slowing down. I couldn't make her keep up her speed. She tired real quick."

"It doesn't make sense," Crystal said. She looked at the horse's hooves to make sure she hadn't lost a shoe. She couldn't find anything wrong with the horse.

"Leon, load the horse into Mr. Rice's trailer," said Crystal's father.

"Wait, Dad, Crystal said. "Maybe there was something wrong with Havana Rose."

Miguel Diaz looked straight into his daughter's eyes, eyes that were so like his own. He stood up, tall and proud. "It was a horse race, darling. We lost. We do not make excuses. We pay our bets." Miguel motioned Leon to go on.

Crystal knew better than to argue with her father. He could have a mean temper sometimes. She turned and headed for the barn. She just couldn't watch as her father's favorite horse was loaded into the trailer. It was too sad.

"Crystal. Hey, Crystal, wait!" called Bobby Lee. He ran toward her.

Crystal didn't want to talk to Bobby Lee or hear him brag about winning. Then suddenly he was by her side.

"Look, I'm sorry about your daddy's

horse," said Bobby Lee. He looked serious.

"Well, I didn't see you slowing your horse to let our horse win," Crystal said. She knew she wasn't being fair, but she was too upset to stop herself.

"I couldn't do that, Crystal. I had to give it my best. I just thought Havana Rose would beat Southern Pride. I'm as surprised as you are. Anyway, be glad it was Havana Rose you lost and not your horse, Chance." His voice was suddenly a whisper. "Chance is the horse my daddy really wants."

Crystal was shocked.

"Bobby Lee! Let's go, boy," Mr. Rice yelled. He climbed into his big, shiny black car.

"Look, I'll call you, Crystal. We'll go see a movie or something," Bobby Lee said. He smiled and then ran to his father's car.

Crystal watched as Bobby Lee got

into the car. Mr. Rice roared out of the parking area with the horse truck and trailer following close behind.

She wondered how she could still care for Bobby Lee, but she did. He didn't visit her in rehab. Now he had helped *his* father take *her* father's horse. Tears filled her eyes. She wiped them away with her hands.

She heard her father calling her to come to the house, but she didn't want to go in just yet. She walked into the barn. It was cool inside and smelled of hay.

Chance stuck his head out of his stall. He bobbed his head as Crystal walked to him. "Hello, boy." Crystal reached and scratched her horse's head.

She remembered Bobby Lee's words, especially the part about his father wanting her horse. "Well, that isn't going to happen, Chance. No way," Crystal promised. She leaned her head against her horse's neck.

"I'm sorry, Miss Diaz," Leon said. He quietly walked to the stall.

Crystal whirled around. "Don't do that, Leon! And don't call me Miss Diaz."

"Okay, but don't do what?" Leon asked. He didn't know what she was talking about.

"Don't sneak up on me," Crystal said. "Did you want something?"

Leon shifted his weight from one foot to the other. He didn't look at her. "I feel like I let your father down and you, too. I'm a good rider, really. I've won a lot of races in Cuba."

Leon looked so unhappy that Crystal felt sorry for him. She reached out and touched his arm. "Like my father said, it was a race and our horse lost."

"I just keep thinking if I'd done something different . . ." Leon said softly. He looked at Crystal as if he were trying to figure her out.

"Forget it. Let's go to the house and get something cold to drink," she smiled. *He's not really so bad*, she thought as she walked next to him down the length of the barn.

Passing Havana Rose's empty stall, Crystal stopped to close the bottom door. She saw something silver shining in the stall. Curious, she went in and reached into the hay that covered the floor. She pulled out a feed bucket.

"What's this doing in here?" Crystal asked, holding up the bucket. "You didn't feed the horse before the race, did you?"

"No way. If you feed a horse before a race, it can't run fast. Everyone knows that," Leon said angrily.

"Well, how did this bucket get in this stall?" Crystal frowned.

"Maybe it has been in there a while and no one noticed," Leon said.

Or maybe someone tried to hide the bucket under the hay, Crystal thought.

36

Chapter 5

At breakfast the next day, Crystal tried to tell her father about the bucket and what she was thinking. "If Havana Rose had just eaten a bucketful of oats, it would explain why she lost."

Miguel pushed his chair back from the table and stood up. "Sweetheart, I know you are sad we lost the race. So am I. But no one cheated. I think you watch too many crime shows on TV." He winked at Donya, who was standing at the sink washing dishes.

"I need some money for grocery shopping today, Miguel. There is no money in the checking account," said Aunt Donya. She didn't look at Crystal's questioning eyes.

Miguel gave Donya a look like he didn't want her talking about money in front of his daughter.

Miguel gave Aunt Donya two twenty-dollar bills. "I'll transfer some more money into that account today," Miguel said. He gave Donya a look like he didn't want her talking about money in front of his daughter.

Crystal looked at the brace on her leg and knew why her father was having money troubles. *It's my fault*, she thought. The hospital bills had been more than their insurance policy would pay. "Dad, I'm sorry."

Miguel looked at Crystal with surprise. "These money problems are not your fault. The farm didn't have a good year. But we will be all right." He smiled at Crystal. Then he went out the kitchen door toward his office.

Crystal watched her father walk across the yard, and then she turned to her aunt. "It *is* my fault. The accident, the extra vet bills for Chance. And he had to hire Leon to do my chores."

"No, no. Don't think like that. You are home now. Everything will get better, you'll see," said Aunt Donya.

"Yeah, right. What good am I with this bad leg?" Crystal cried. She was feeling sorry for herself. She stood up and limped to the kitchen door.

"Don't forget, you promised to go shopping with me," Donya said.

"I'll be in the barn," Crystal answered. She let the door bang shut behind her. The last thing she wanted to do was go into town where she might see some of her friends, or worse, Bobby Lee Rice.

After spending an hour brushing Chance, Crystal went into town with her aunt. The first stop was the local grocery store. Crystal wanted to stay in the car, but her aunt wouldn't let her. Aunt Donya said it was time that Crystal got out and spoke to people, and the grocery store would be a good place to start.

Crystal hated the way the checkers and other people in the store looked at her as if she was a doll who might break.

She was glad when they finished shopping and got back to the car. As her Aunt Donya put the grocery bags in the trunk, Crystal leaned against the car. "You sure bought a lot of black beans and rice."

Donya laughed. "It's cheap. Besides, I feel like cooking some good Cuban food. Black beans, rice, and fried bananas are your daddy's favorite foods. Should cheer him up."

"Don't you mean, make him forget his money troubles? This is all my fault," Crystal said. She slid into the passenger seat.

Donya drove down the main street of the small town. As they got close to the bank, Crystal saw Mr. Rice standing on the sidewalk talking to Brock Lee, the town's only deputy. "Please pull over, Aunt Donya. I want to talk to Mr. Rice," Crystal said.

Donya slowed the car and then turned into a parking space. "What do you have to talk about with that man?"

"A horse," said Crystal. She slammed the car door and limped over to Mr. Rice.

"Good morning, little lady," said

Mr. Rice as Crystal reached him. Brock Lee tipped his cowboy hat and grinned.

Crystal had known the deputy most of her life. She and her friends liked to call him "Broccoli" when they knew he couldn't hear them.

Crystal nodded at the deputy, then turned her full attention on Mr. Rice. "Bobby Lee says you really want my horse, Chance. Well, I've got an idea you might be interested in."

Mr. Rice smiled, taking her seriously for the moment. "What's your big idea, little lady?"

Crystal looked at Brock Lee. She didn't want him to hear her idea. He had a big mouth, and before sunset, everyone in town would know her plan. He wasn't leaving, so she took a deep breath before speaking. "I've got a bet for you. I race Chance against your son Bobby Lee on Southern Pride. If I win, you stamp my daddy's mortgage paid and give back our horse

Havana Rose. If I lose, you get my horse, Chance."

"Well, that's a good handicap for you, Mr. Rice," Brock Lee said with a chuckle. He looked down at Crystal's leg in the brace so everyone would know what he meant.

Crystal became angry. "I may have a brace on my leg, 'Broccoli,' but that doesn't mean I'm handicapped or that I can't still ride."

Crystal figured since Mr. Rice was a gambler, he'd like the odds of her having a handicap. *He probably thinks there is no way I can win with my bad leg,* Crystal thought.

Mr. Rice grinned like he was enjoying himself. He stuck his thumbs in the sides of his vest, puffing out his chest. *He looks like a rooster ready to crow*, thought Crystal.

"Little lady, you got yourself a bet," said Mr. Rice. He winked at the deputy.

"I may need a couple of weeks to get ready," Crystal said. She turned toward the car.

Mr. Rice chuckled. "You take all the time you need." Crystal stepped carefully off the sidewalk and then limped to the car.

As Donya drove out of town, she asked Crystal what she'd done.

Crystal didn't answer. She was wondering the same thing. She just agreed to a horse race, which meant having to ride Chance again. She shivered in the hot car.

Chapter 6

At first, it wasn't easy for Crystal to get back on Chance. She was nervous, which made her horse jumpy, too. She worked with Chance in the coolness of the early mornings and then again at dusk. She remembered everything she knew about riding. By the end of the first week, Crystal was ready to let Chance gallop as fast as he could go.

As she rode Chance around the track, Crystal saw her father and Leon standing by the fence. They both stopped what they were doing to watch her. Rounding the turn, she slowed Chance to a trot. She could see her father smiling. She knew he was glad she was riding again. Leon was grinning, too. He held up her leg brace like it was a trophy.

"What are you doing with my brace?" Crystal asked. She pulled Chance to a stop.

Leon put the brace back on the mounting block. "Nothing. I got so excited seeing you galloping, I just picked it up."

For a second, Crystal wondered if Leon was telling the truth. *Maybe he has a reason for reminding me of my handicap. By why would he?* she thought. *He's been so helpful and kind.* She shook her head to clear her thoughts.

"Here, let me help you down," said Crystal's father. He reached up and grabbed her by the waist. He carefully set her down on the mounting block step where she could put her brace back on. Leon grabbed Chance's reins and led the horse back to the barn.

"I wish you would forget about this race," Crystal's father said. "Things are getting better on the farm. We got two more yearlings in today for training."

"I can't forget about it. A bet is a bet," Crystal said. She stood up and looked her father straight in the eyes. "Besides, I know Chance can beat Southern Pride."

"I thought Havana Rose could beat Southern Pride." Her father stared across the track at the green meadows in the distance.

"I still think someone fed our horse right before the race."

"That's crazy. No one cheated in the race," her father said.

Crystal was going to argue some more when she saw Bobby Lee's blue pickup drive into the barn parking area. *I wonder what he wants*, she thought. Her heart began beating faster.

Her father waved at Bobby Lee, then headed into the house. Crystal watched as Bobby Lee walked toward her with a big grin on his face.

"Crystal," Bobby Lee said. He pushed his cowboy hat back off his forehead. "You still want to go through with this race?"

"I gave my word to your father," Crystal said. She loved Bobby Lee's blue eyes. She thought they were the color of a spring sky.

"It doesn't matter what you said to my daddy. I'm asking you if you really want to have this race. I know how much Chance means to you," Bobby Lee said. He looked serious.

Crystal just stared at him. "What makes you think I won't beat you, Bobby Lee?"

Bobby Lee grinned and shrugged. "Well, for one thing, I'm a better rider. Second, I've been racing all summer and you've only been at it a week now."

"I'm ready to race you tomorrow," Crystal said. "I don't need all summer to get in shape. So maybe you'd better go home and give that Southern Pride a workout." She let her temper make her speak without thinking.

"I don't want to race you, Crystal," Bobby Lee said. "But if you insist, then we'll race. What I really came here for was to ask you if you wanted to go to Lexington tonight and listen to some bluegrass music."

Crystal's heart beat faster. There was nothing she wanted more than to go out with Bobby Lee, but not the night before the race.

She looked at him and wondered if he had a reason for wanting her to go with him to Lexington. She still couldn't stop thinking that someone had fed Havana Rose an extra bucket of oats. "I'll see you tomorrow morning at the starting gate, Bobby Lee."

Later, after her father and aunt had gone to bed, Crystal quietly left the house. The lights from two lamp posts shined on the house and barn. Crystal looked up at the full moon. She thought of the song "Blue Moon of Kentucky." She smiled. She could smell the night-blooming jasmine and hear the crickets calling to each other in the tall grass.

In the barn, Crystal went straight to Chance's stall. The horse nickered and nudged her shoulder like he was glad to see her. "I'm staying here with you tonight, buddy. I'll make sure no one does any funny stuff."

She pulled a saddle blanket off the door and threw it on the hay. *I'm not really going to sleep*, she told herself. But she curled up in the blanket and fell asleep.

Late in the night, Crystal woke up. She thought she heard something. She got up and looked out of the stall. Shadows moved along the barn floor. "Who's there?" Crystal asked. No one answered. A door squeaked in one of the stalls, then all was quiet.

Chapter 7

The next morning, Crystal was nervous. She had stayed awake most of the night, wondering if someone was in the barn after she woke up. When Leon came to saddle Chance, Crystal asked him if he'd been in the barn the night before.

"No, I didn't leave the bunkhouse all night. When I sleep, I sleep hard. Looks like you slept out here though," Leon said. He picked a piece of straw from Crystal's hair.

"Yeah, nervous I guess," Crystal said. She did not want to tell him why she decided to sleep in the barn.

"I'll saddle Chance and bring him out if you want to go up to the house and get cleaned up," Leon said. He led the horse from the stall.

Crystal combed her long brown hair with her fingers then pulled it into a ponytail. "I think I'll just stay with my horse until after the race."

Leon gave her a sharp look, and then shrugged. He quickly saddled Chance. "You want me to lead him out to the track?"

Crystal picked up the horse's reins. "No, I can do it. Go on ahead. I'll catch up."

Leading Chance, Crystal walked straight to the racetrack. Mr. Rice and Bobby Lee were already at the starting gate with their horse Southern Pride. Suddenly, Crystal's father and aunt were by her side.

"There's still time to call off this race, sweetheart," said her father. Crystal thought they looked worried, which only made her want to race even more.

"I don't plan to lose," Crystal said. Her voice had more confidence than she was feeling.

"Where is your brace?" Aunt Donya asked.

"In the barn. I can't wear it when I ride. Now stop worrying, both of you," Crystal said.

Within minutes, Crystal and Bobby Lee were sitting on their horses at the starting line. Crystal shook her head, trying to relax. She'd raced Bobby Lee a hundred times in the past just for fun, but that was before her accident, before the bet.

"You're looking fierce and determined this morning, Crystal," said Bobby Lee. He grinned at her like he wasn't worried about the race or anything.

Crystal frowned at him, wondering why he couldn't just shut up and leave her alone to concentrate. *Maybe that's his plan*, she told herself. *He thinks that*

Crystal leaned forward, placing her weight over the horse's center of gravity.

big smile of his will make me forget what I'm supposed to be doing.

"Riders ready," Crystal's father said. He held up a blue flag.

Crystal leaned forward, placing her weight over the horse's center of gravity. When the flag dropped, they were off. The two horses were almost even with each other as they raced down the track. Coming around the backside, Bobby Lee took the lead.

"Come on, Chance, we'll take him in the turn," Crystal said. She urged her horse to go faster and faster until she felt like they were almost flying. Chance passed Southern Pride as though the other horse was standing still. Crystal kept her eyes on the finish line. She watched it come closer and closer until they were over it. Chance beat Southern Pride by a full horse length.

Crystal heard her father and aunt cheering. She looked in their direction and saw Mr. Rice giving Leon an angry look. *That's odd*, she thought. She was surprised that they knew each other.

"I won!" Crystal shouted. She couldn't remember ever being so happy. She looked down at her bad leg. She thought for the first time since the accident that maybe she was going to be okay after all.

Her father helped her down from the horse. "You were magic. You rode like the wind," said Crystal's father.

Crystal's dark eyes glowed with happiness. She turned to Mr. Rice, who looked madder than she had ever seen. "I guess my handicap didn't get in my way," Crystal said. She remembered his joke with the deputy. "Will you bring Havana Rose back here this afternoon?"

"I'll have one of my men see to it," Mr. Rice said. His voice was angry. It was clear to everyone that he didn't like losing. "Come on, Bobby Lee, let's get out of here."

Ignoring his father, Bobby Lee slid off his horse and came over to Crystal. "That was some great riding, girl," he said. "Of course, I slowed Southern Pride to help you out."

Crystal was angry. "That's not true! I saw you come over the finish line. You and your horse were winded from trying to catch up."

Bobby Lee laughed and held up his hands as if he was giving up. "Okay, I admit I tried my best to win. You won fair and square."

"Which is more than I can say about you when you raced Leon," Crystal said. She grabbed Chance's reins and started walking toward the barn.

"What are you talking about?" Bobby Lee asked.

Crystal didn't answer. As she and Bobby Lee were about to pass the Rice's horse trailer, they heard Mr. Rice arguing with someone.

"I paid you a lot of money to feed the girl's horse right before the race. Now, I want to know what happened," Mr. Rice said.

"I'm telling you, Crystal slept with her horse. She didn't leave it alone for a second," said the voice.

Crystal and Bobby Lee looked at each other. They seemed to be thinking the same thing. They stepped around the horse trailer, coming face to face with Mr. Rice and Leon.

"Daddy, did you cheat in that first race with Havana Rose and Southern Pride?" Bobby Lee asked. He stared at his father with disbelief and disgust.

Mr. Rice's face turned red and he seemed at a loss for words.

"What about you, Leon?" Crystal asked. "Is this how you repay my father's kindness, by feeding our horse so it will lose?" She couldn't believe she had thought Leon was a nice guy.

Crystal's father walked up. "Is this

true, Leon? You cheated in the first race and were planning to cheat in this one, too?"

Leon didn't say anything. He just shrugged like it was no big deal.

"I want you off my property, Leon. Get your things and get out," said Crystal's father. He turned to Mr. Rice. "I can understand why Leon did it. He needs money. What I don't understand are your reasons, Mr. Rice. You're a rich man. You don't need to cheat."

"You can't prove anything," Mr. Rice said.

"No, I can't. But I want you to honor your bet," Miguel said. He looked Mr. Rice straight in the eyes.

"Fine. Your Havana Rose will be returned this afternoon. Your mortgage will be stamped *paid*," said Mr. Rice. He walked to his car and was about to get in when he turned back to his son. "Come on, Bobby Lee."

Bobby Lee shook his head *no*. Mr.

Rice got into his car and slammed the door. Seconds later, he raced his car down the driveway. The driver of the Rices' horse trailer followed.

"I'll put Chance in his stall," said Crystal's father. Miguel led the horse away, leaving Crystal and Bobby Lee alone.

Crystal felt bad for Bobby Lee, who stood there looking like he couldn't believe what just happened. She'd never seen him look so sad. She also felt guilty for blaming him when all along it was Leon. "You know, Bobby Lee, I think I'd like to go hear some bluegrass music tonight."

Bobby Lee looked at her. He looked embarrassed. "Are you sure you want to go with me after what my daddy did?"

Crystal smiled. "*You* didn't do anything. You can't help how your daddy is anymore than I can help limping on my bad leg."

"I don't think your leg was much of a handicap today, Crystal. You rode like a champion," Bobby Lee said. He was feeling better already.

"I sure did. I beat you good, Bobby Lee. And I'll do it again," Crystal teased.

Bobby Lee grinned. "Oh, yeah?"

Crystal laughed. "Yeah. Come on, let's go have some of Aunt Donya's famous pecan pie and you can tell me why you think you'll win next time."

Bobby Lee took Crystal's hand. Together, they walked toward the ranch house.

Artesian Press

High Interest...Easy Reading

Multicultural Read-Alongs

Standing Tall Mystery Series

Mystery chapter books that portray young ethnic Americans as they meet challenges, solve puzzles, and arrive at solutions. By doing the right thing the mystery falls away and they are revealed to have been...Standing Tall!

Set 1	Book	Cassette	CD
Don't Look Now or Ever			
	1-58659-084-7	1-58659-094-4	1-58659-266-1
Ghost Biker	1-58659-082-0	1-58659-092-8	1-58659-265-3
The Haunted Hound	1-58659-085-5	1-58659-095-2	1-58659-267-X
The Howling House	1-58659-083-9	1-58659-093-6	1-58659-269-6
The Twin	1-58659-081-2	1-58659-091-X	1-58659-268-8
Set 2			
As the Eagle Goes	1-58659-086-3	1-58659-096-0	1-58659-270-X
Beyond Glory	1-58659-087-1	1-58659-097-9	1-58659-271-8
Shadow on the Snow	1-58659-088-X	1-58659-098-7	1-58659-272-6
Terror on Tulip Lane	1-58659-089-8	1-58659-099-5	1-58659-273-4
The Vanished One	1-58659-100-2	1-58659-090-1	1-58659-274-2
Set 3			
Back From the Grave	1-58659-101-0	1-58659-106-1	1-58659-345-5
Guilt	1-58659-103-7	1-58659-108-8	1-58659-347-1
Treasure In the Keys	1-58659-102-9	1-58659-107-X	1-58659-346-3
"I Didn't Do It!"	1-58659-104-5	1-58659-109-6	1-58659-348-X
Of Home and Heart	1-58659-105-3	1-58659-110-X	1-58659-349-8

www.artesianpress.com

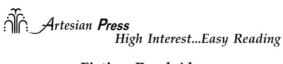

Artesian Press
High Interest...Easy Reading

Fiction Read-Alongs

Take 10 Books

Mystery	Books	Cassette	CD
Nobody Lives in Apartment N-2			
	1-58659-001-4	1-58659-006-5	1-58659-275-0
Return of the Eagle	1-58659-002-2	1-58659-007-3	1-58659-276-9
Touchdown	1-58659-003-0	1-58659-008-1	1-58659-277-7
Stick Like Glue	1-58659-004-9	1-58659-009-x	1-58659-278-5
Freeze Frame	1-58659-005-7	1-58659-010-3	1-58659-279-3
Adventure			
Cliffhanger	1-58659-011-1	1-58659-016-2	1-58659-280-7
The Great UFO Frame-Up			
	1-58659-012-x	1-58659-016-2	1-58659-281-5
Swamp Furies	1-58659-013-8	1-58659-018-9	1-58659-282-3
The Seal Killers	1-58659-014-6	1-58659-019-7	1-58659-283-1
Mean Waters	1-58659-015-4	1-58659-020-0	1-58659-284-x
Sports			
The Phantom Falcon	1-58659-031-6	1-58659-036-7	1-58659-290-4
Half and Half	1-58659-032-4	1-58659-037-5	1-58659-291-2
Knucklehead	1-58659-033-2	1-58659-038-3	1-58659-292-0
The Big Sundae	1-58659-034-0	1-58659-039-0	1-58659-293-9
Match Point	1-58659-035-9	1-58659-040-5	1-58659-294-7
Chillers			
Alien Encounter	1-58659-051-0	1-58659-056-1	1-58659-295-5
Ghost in the Desert	1-58659-052-9	1-58659-057-x	1-58659-296-3
The Huanted Beach House			
	1-58659-053-7	1-58659-058-8	1-58659-297-1
Trapped in the Sixties	1-58659-054-5	1-58659-059-6	1-58659-298-x
The Water Witch	1-58659-055-3	1-58659-060-x	1-58659-299-8
Thrillers			
Bronco Buster	1-58659-041-3	1-58659-046-4	1-58659-325-0
The Climb	1-58659-042-1	1-58659-047-2	1-58659-326-9
Search and Rescue	1-58659-043-x	1-58659-048-0	1-58659-327-7
Timber	1-58659-044-8	1-58659-048-0	1-58659-328-5
Tough Guy	1-58659-045-6	1-58659-050-2	1-58659-329-3
Fantasy			
The Cooler King	1-58659-061-8	1-58659-066-9	1-58659-330-7
Ken and the Samurai	1-58659-062-6	1-58659-067-7	1-58659-331-5
The Rabbit Tattoo	1-58659-063-4	1-58659-068-5	1-58659-332-2
Under the Waterfall	1-58659-064-2	1-58659-069-3	1-58659-333-1
Horror			
The Indian Hills Horror	1-58659-072-3	1-58659-077-4	1-58659-335-8
From the Eye of the Cat	1-58659-071-5	1-58659-076-6	1-58659-336-6
The Oak Tree Horror	1-58659-073-1	1-58659-078-2	1-58659-337-4
Return to Gallows Hill	1-58659-075-8	1-58659-080-4	1-58659-338-2
The Pack	1-58659-074-x	1-58659-079-0	1-58659-339-0
Romance			
Connie's Secret	1-58659-460-5	1-58659-915-1	1-58659-340-4
Crystal's Chance	1-58659-459-1	1-58659-917-8	1-58659-341-2
Bad Luck Boy	1-58659-458-3	1-58659-916-x	1-58659-342-0
A Summer Romance	1-58659-140-1	1-58659-918-6	1-58659-343-9
To Nicole With Love	1-58659-188-6	1-58659-919-4	1-58659-344-7

www.artesianpress.com